Museum
Kittens

Remembering the original Boris! – HW

For Dizzie and Billy-Bob – SL

STRIPES PUBLISHING LIMITED
An imprint of the Little Tiger Group
1 Coda Studios, 189 Munster Road,
London SW6 6AW

Imported into the EEA by Penguin Random House Ireland,
Morrison Chambers, 32 Nassau Street, Dublin D02 YH68

A paperback original
First published in Great Britain in 2021

Text copyright © Holly Webb, 2021
Illustrations copyright © Sarah Lodge, 2021
Author photograph copyright © Charlotte Knee Photography

ISBN: 978-1-78895-327-6

MIX
Paper from
responsible sources
FSC® C020471

The Forest Stewardship Council® (FSC®) is a global, not-for-profit organization
dedicated to the promotion of responsible forest management worldwide. FSC®
defines standards based on agreed principles for responsible forest stewardship
that are supported by environmental, social, and economic stakeholders.
To learn more, visit www.fsc.org

10 9 8 7 6 5 4 3 2 1

Museum
Kittens

The Treasure Map

Holly Webb

Illustrated by Sarah Lodge

LITTLE TIGER

LONDON

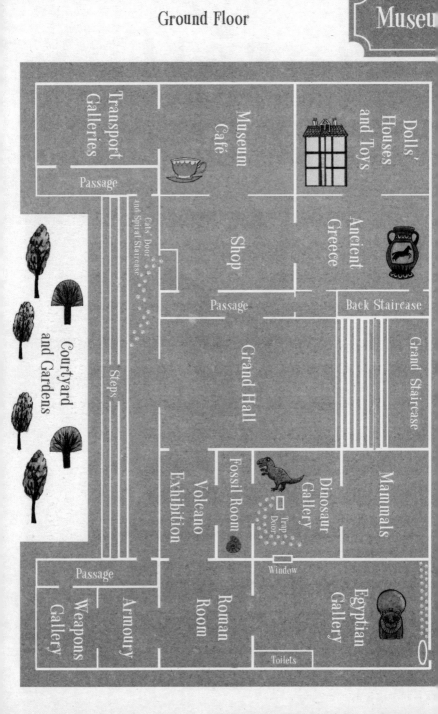

Ground Floor

Museu

Transport Galleries

Museum Cafe

Dolls' Houses and Toys

Passage

Ancient Greece

Shop

Cats' Door and Spiral Staircase

Passage

Back Staircase

Courtyard and Gardens

Grand Hall

Steps

Grand Staircase

Fossil Room

Mammals

Volcano Exhibition

Dinosaur Gallery

Trap Door

Window

Passage

Armoury

Roman Room

Egyptian Gallery

Weapons Gallery

Toilets

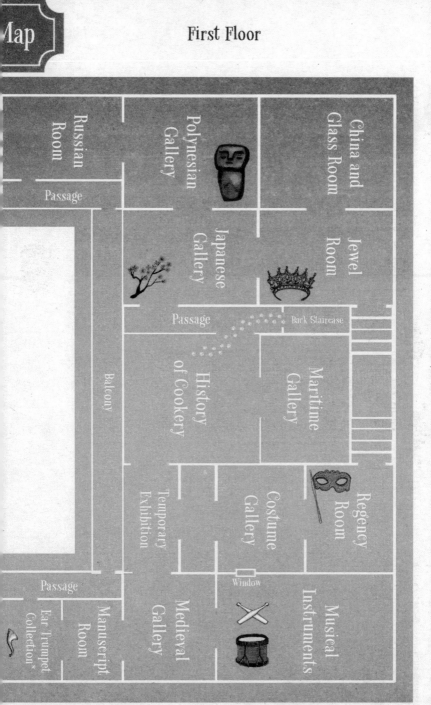

Map

First Floor

Russian Room

Passage

Polynesian Gallery

China and Glass Room

Jewel Room

Japanese Gallery

Passage

Back Staircase

Balcony

History of Cookery

Maritime Gallery

Temporary Exhibition

Costume Gallery

Regency Room

Passage

Manuscript Room

Medieval Gallery

Window

Musical Instruments

Ear Trumpet Collection*

Chapter One

"Look, there's a dragon!" Tasha mewed
excitedly, her tabby tail bushing out
as she stared up at the floating clouds.
"I can see its wings, and there's smoke
coming out of its nostrils!"

Bianca, Tasha's white-furred sister,
rolled on to her back and opened one eye
to peer at the sky. "You really do have the
most incredible imagination. It's a cloud."

1

"I can see a dragon," Peter said, looking hopefully at Tasha. He wasn't quite sure that he could, but he loved Tasha's stories. He was warming his black fur in a lovely patch of sun and he quite fancied hearing about a dragon.

The kittens had been sent up to the roof of the museum by their mother, to shoo away any pigeons that thought it was a good place to build their nests. The museum cats' main job was to protect the precious treasures from rats and mice, but pigeons were a problem too. They were messy – they dropped feathers everywhere and they had a nasty habit of dropping other things too, sometimes on visitors. Grandpa Ivan, who had been guarding the museum for longer than anyone could remember, said that pigeons were just rats with wings. He also said that squirrels were just rats in fancy coats.

Luckily, the kittens hadn't spotted so much as a stray feather up on the roof – nothing but warm roof tiles and sunny patches, perfect for an afternoon doze.

Boris yawned and stretched in the sun, then he sat up and eyed the racing clouds too. "That's not a dragon." He scrambled to his feet, the tip of his tail twitching with excitement. "That's a sailing ship!"

"You're worse than she is," Bianca muttered, wriggling a little to move her ears out of the sun. They were a very delicate pink and burned if she wasn't careful. "It's a cloud and nothing else."

"Oh, Bianca," Tasha said sadly, staring at her sister. "Can't you see anything?"

"Clouds…"

"Shhh, you two!" Boris demanded. "This is important."

Both his sisters turned and glared at him, but Boris was so fascinated by the shapes in the sky that he didn't even notice. He was standing on the very ridge of the roof now, the wind ruffling his stripy ginger fur and blowing back his whiskers. "Look at that ship go! Where do you think it's sailing to?"

Bianca, Tasha and Peter exchanged glances and then sighed. Boris was usually rather lazy, but every so often he would get very excited about something. Most of the time it was food. When the museum café had brought out a prawn sandwich special, Boris had moved out of their cellar home and set up camp outside the café's back door.

Now his golden eyes were sparkling and his tail was whipping back and forth. He was in one of those moods again. And somehow that always meant a great deal of fuss and work for the other kittens…

"I could be a ship's cat … an adventurer! I'd sail across the seven seas and live on an island!"

"I think you only end up living on

an island if your ship sinks," Peter said thoughtfully. "It's not something you *want* to happen."

But Boris wasn't listening. "Think of all the fish!" He peered up at the sky and huffed sadly. "I'll never catch that ship." Then his eyes widened and he leaped round, the fur standing up along his spine. "There's a ship in the museum! Come on! No more lazing around in the sun, we're going adventuring!" He started to scramble down the tiles to the little round window that led into the curators' office.

"Do we have to?" Bianca mewed crossly. "I've only just got comfortable."

"I think we should," Tasha replied. "You never know what he'll do when he's like this."

Bianca huffed, and stood up, picking her way down the tiles with finicky paws. Tasha and Peter hurried after her and peered through the round window. They were just in time to see a ginger tail tip vanish out of the office doorway.

"He must be heading for *The Silver Lion!*" Tasha said, galloping over the dusty boards.

"The what?" Peter called.

"It's the name of the ship – haven't we shown it to you yet?"

Peter had only come to live at the museum a short time ago, after living on the streets for the first months of his life. He kept thinking he'd explored the whole of the huge building, but then the other kittens would point out a new corridor full of galleries that he'd missed.

"No… Is it an actual ship?"

"Yes! It's a galleon, and it's about four hundred years old. It's in a dry dock built at the back of the museum," Tasha called out as they scampered down the back stairs, the ones that weren't used by the museum visitors. "We can get to it through the Maritime Gallery."

Peter wasn't sure what a dry dock was, but Tasha clearly expected him to know, so he didn't say anything. He would find out soon, he supposed. They scooted across a corridor and squeezed along a narrow gap behind a row of glass cases full of sailors' uniforms. Peter could hear Bianca puffing and grumbling behind him.

"Sun is good for my fur… And it makes

my whiskers curl.
I don't want to go and
hang around ancient boats…"

"There, look!" Tasha peeped
round a huge doorway, and Peter gasped.
The Silver Lion loomed above them,
filling a huge gallery that was several
storeys high. She was surrounded by glass
walkways and bridges with railings on
either side, so that the visitors could see
close up without damaging the fragile
woodwork. Since the kittens had come out

on the first floor, they were about level with the main deck.

The ship was built of wood, but it had aged to a silvery grey, with faint traces of faded paint here and there. The very front of the ship curved up into an enormous lion carved on to the prow, its paws stretched to leap out over the water.

Boris was lurking behind a display board, trying not to let the visitors spot him, and the three other kittens nudged in too.

"Isn't she beautiful?" he sighed.

Bianca looked round jealously. "Who?"

"The ship! *The Silver Lion!* I wish she still had her sails. She ought to be out on the river, not stuck here in a dry dock." He peered round the board. "There's no one looking. Come on!" He shot out from their hiding place and raced up the walkway to the main deck.

"Get after him!" Bianca hissed, dashing along the walkway with Tasha and Peter close behind. The three kittens skidded after Boris, keeping an eye out for visitors – but luckily the huge gallery was empty.

Boris stood in the centre of the floor, his nose in the air.

"It smells of the sea," he said wistfully, gazing around. The other kittens exchanged glances.

"It smells *old*..." Peter said doubtfully. "I can't smell any sea." He'd seen Boris being enthusiastic about swords and armour, but this was different. Boris looked a bit like Tasha when she was in the middle of one of her best stories, dreamy and excited all at the same time.

"It smells like adventure… Hey, what was that?" Boris demanded, whirling round. "Did you hear it?"

The other kittens pricked their ears and twitched their tails, listening hard.

Down in the depths of the ship there came the *tap-tap-tapping* of little ratty paws.

🐾 Chapter Two 🐾

"Rats!" Boris hissed. "Rats on our ship!"
He ducked under the railings around the
glass walkway, his tail fluffed to about
three times its usual size.

"Come back!" Tasha squeaked. She
leaped after him, trying to grab him back,
but she was too late – Boris was already
standing on the four-hundred-year-old
timbers of the main deck.

"Er, Boris," Peter whispered anxiously. "I don't think you're supposed to do that."

"He's definitely *not* supposed to do that," Bianca said, looking extremely prim. "That is absolutely *forbidden*!"

"Oh, Boris, be careful! The timbers are so delicate," Tasha wailed.

"Rats, Tasha! What's the most important thing we're supposed to do as museum cats?" Boris called back. "We chase rats away! They're in the ship! We have to protect it. Come on." He settled into a stalking crouch and crept across the deck, whiskers twitching as he tracked the scrabbly noises.

"We can't let him face up against the rats on his own," Peter said, turning to Bianca and Tasha. "Some of them are even bigger than he is."

"But it's a precious museum exhibit!" Tasha put one paw through the gap in the railings and then drew it back again, wincing.

"It's survived this long," Peter pointed out. "We have to go, Tasha. We can't stay here – listen! There are visitors coming."

Tasha looked round worriedly. Peter was right – she could hear footsteps and voices. The kittens weren't supposed to be running around the galleries when the museum was open – if they were spotted they'd be in all sorts of trouble.

"And he's right about the rats," Peter added. "Who knows what they could be planning? They might be nibbling holes in the timbers."

At that Tasha gave a squeak of horror and shot through the railings on to the deck of the ship. Peter and Bianca slunk after her, just as a group of visitors came tramping up the walkway.

"Quick, through here," Boris hissed over his shoulder as he headed into a dark doorway at the bow. "I can hear them!"

All four kittens crouched tensely, listening hard.

From far down below came squeaky little rat voices, floating up through a square opening in the floor.

Four brave rats on a pirate ship
Yo ho ho and a hunk of cheese!
We'll soon have that treasure in our grip
Yo ho ho and a hunk of cheese!

"Are they *singing*?" Bianca asked, her blue eyes glittering in the darkness. "What are they wittering on about?"

"It's from a book," Tasha said. "Although they've changed the words around. I suppose rats just don't like rum. And really, I don't think this is a pirate ship—"

"Of course it is!" Boris whipped round, his whiskers bristling. "Now shhh, they're coming – get ready to leap on them!"

The rats were marching merrily up the ladder from the lower decks, their scratchy footsteps keeping time with their song.

The treasure, our treasure, oh my,
oh yes!
Yo ho ho and a hunk of cheese!
Those clumsy cats will never guess!
Yo ho ho and a hunk of cheese!

Boris drew himself back, ready to spring as the first rat whiskers came whiffling through the square opening. He could feel the three other kittens behind him, too excited even to breathe. He was just about to launch himself on the first dastardly rat, when he realized exactly *what* the rats were singing.

Treasure? What treasure?

"Hang on…" He skittered backwards, shooing the others into the shadows against the wooden wall.

"Why?"

"What are we doing?"

"Boris, you—"

"Shhh! Listen," Boris interrupted. "It's important. Get behind that barrel, we mustn't let them see us."

Up the ladder came the first of the rats, a big brown one that Boris had bashed noses with a few weeks before.

"Come on, you lot!" he said. "We have to find the treasure before those horrible cats get their grubby paws on it!"

Boris heard Bianca suck in her breath and then she whispered faintly, "Grubby? *Grubby?* From a rat? How dare he?"

"Treasure, Bianca," he hissed in her ear. "Shhh."

The kittens listened closely as all four

of the little rat gang marched up the ladder and out on to the deck.

"But, Luther, it's all very well saying there's treasure. It's no good if we don't know where it is," said a light brown rat.

"Shut up, Morris. You know your problem? No ambition. No drive. You lot are lucky you've got me to sort you out. You'd be nowhere without me, nowhere. Isn't that right, Pip?"

One of the two smaller rats nodded, his whiskers quivering. The other, whose fur was a pale grey, sighed loudly.

"What was that?" The huge rat rounded on her. "Did you say something, Dusty?"

"No, boss."

"I should think not. Come on. The treasure awaits! It's hidden somewhere in the museum and we're going to be the ones to find it, as soon as we've worked out which way up this map goes."

"Follow them!" Boris growled. "But quietly! We mustn't let them see that we know what they know."

"We *don't* know what they know!" Peter said, his ears flattening in confusion.

"We know they know *something*!" Boris snapped back. "It definitely looked like they had a map!"

"Er…" Tasha peered out across the deck.

"Oh, don't you start arguing too!" Boris slunk out from behind the barrel and looked around. "Hang on – where did they go?"

"That's what I was trying to tell you," Tasha sighed. "They've gone. Disappeared."

The three other kittens slipped out on to the deck beside Boris.

"They can't have disappeared," Boris

muttered. "We were only seconds behind them. Noooo... I don't believe it!"

"They probably have their own secret tunnels in and out of the ship," Tasha pointed out with a shudder. "Now we need to get out of here, before someone sees us. One of the museum staff, or worse, Ma or Grandpa Ivan! It's all very well saying we were chasing the rats, but there isn't even a sniff of a rat here now, is there?"

Boris sighed. "All right. Let's head to the Maritime Gallery. Meet you behind the model ships. We need a council of war!"

The Maritime Gallery was full of paintings of ships, models of ships and bits of ships.

There was a whole wall of figureheads of all shapes and sizes, and the ceiling was festooned with fishing nets. It smelled very slightly of the sea, and all four kittens felt their fur ruffle up in an imaginary sea breeze as they trotted in.

"Why do we have to meet in here?" Bianca complained, licking her shiny white fur straight again. "It's all fishy, and not in a good way."

"Treasure," Boris said firmly as they tucked themselves behind the cabinet full of model ships. "You heard those rats talking about a treasure map! Well, we're not going to let those rascals get their ratty little paws on treasure. Any treasure in this museum belongs to us!"

Tasha eyed him uncertainly. "No, it

doesn't, Boris. It belongs
to the museum."

"Mmm, maybe. But it
definitely doesn't belong to
the rats."

"I don't think there's any treasure
to find," Tasha said thoughtfully. "I
mean, those rats aren't very clever."

There was a freezing sort of silence as all the kittens remembered that the not-very-clever rats had recently managed to trick Bianca and shut her up inside a dolls' house for a whole night.

"Although they're extremely horrible and also very, very lucky," Tasha added quickly. "But I think they might have got the wrong end of someone's tail here. I mean, how did they even find a map?"

"Don't you see?" Boris purred, his whiskers curling with excitement. "*The Silver Lion* was a pirate ship. It belonged to the legendary pirate queen, Diamond Nell. She was fearsome! Adventurous! And very, very sneaky. And she liked cats, everybody knows that. Of course someone like Diamond Nell would leave a secret treasure map behind."

"A pirate?" Bianca rolled her eyes and Peter looked doubtful.

"You're making this up," Tasha said uncertainly. "I've never heard of Diamond Nell."

Boris stuck his nose in the air. "Just because you lot don't know about her, it doesn't mean she isn't real!"

❧ Chapter Three ❧

Tasha was still not convinced that the
treasure the rats were looking for really
existed, but Boris's excitement was
starting to rub off on Bianca and Peter.
Bianca loved anything to do with jewels
and Peter was desperate for an adventure.

That night, all four of them were on
guard in the Jewel Room. Boris, Bianca
and Tasha's mother, Smoke, who drew up

the cats' guard rotas, had decided they were better off working together. She had given Boris a very sharp look and added, "After all, there's three of you and one of him," which Boris felt was very unfair. Not *all* the accidents that happened around the museum were his fault.

The Jewel Room was Bianca's favourite assignment. Boris usually found it rather boring, but tonight he couldn't stop gazing around at all the glittering cabinets. What sort of treasure would the map that the rats had found lead to?

He lay stretched out over a glass cabinet, peering down at a tiny, jewelled model of a carriage. It was made of gold and fascinatingly detailed, with perfect horses carved in some dark crystal. Their harnesses were inlaid with diamonds, and so were the carriage wheels. The initials of some long-ago duke were picked out on the carriage doors in dark blue sapphires. Would there be fabulous jewelled carriages in the pirate treasure?

"Do you think there could be pearls?" Bianca wondered. Usually when they were in the Jewel Room, she was the one sitting on the glass cases admiring the exhibits. Now she was curled up beside the cabinet with her eyes closed, fathoms deep in dreams of treasure. "I've always wanted to see what pearls would look like against my fur."

"I think you'd look better wearing something bright," Peter put in. "Um, what are the red ones called?"

Bianca opened her eyes wide and stared at him in horror. How could he not know something so important? "Rubies, of course!"

"Oh yes. Those."

"One does need very fine fur to wear

rubies…" Bianca murmured to herself, but she looked pleased. "You'd suit a collar of pearls, Peter, I think."

"But we can't be sure there is any treasure," Tasha muttered. "So there's no point imagining what it might be."

Boris looked over at her. "First time I've heard you saying we shouldn't imagine things! Why don't you want there to be any treasure, Tasha?"

"It isn't that! I just don't see how the rats got their paws on a treasure map! How could they have found something like that, when all the museum people never noticed it? All this talk is just getting your hopes up. Look at Bianca – she's off in a world of her own, planning which diamonds to wear when she's sailing on her yacht—"

"Not diamonds for nautical wear, Tasha dear," Bianca put in sleepily. "A narrow gold chain would be tasteful for yachting."

"You see!" Tasha hissed. "I don't want to be the boring one who has to cheer everybody up when you find out the treasure was imaginary!"

Boris snorted loudly. "You're being a misery. And you're enjoying it."

"That isn't true!"

Boris wriggled further over the side of the glass cabinet to peer down at Tasha below him. "You don't like it that I knew about Diamond Nell."

"I still don't know where you found out about her." Tasha frowned. "I'm sure she isn't mentioned in any of the stories in the Maritime Gallery."

Boris wrinkled his muzzle thoughtfully. Where had he first heard about the pirate queen? It certainly wasn't from reading the labels on any exhibits. He preferred to let Tasha read those and tell him the interesting bits. Then he thumped a triumphant paw on the glass, and all the other kittens flinched. "Two of the museum staff were talking about her. She's a legend, they said so."

Tasha sighed. "Boris! That means she isn't real."

"No, it means she's special." Boris shook his head. "Like Grandpa Ivan.

I heard some visitors call him a legend yesterday, because he's been here for so long." He gave Tasha a pitying look. "You really ought to know that."

"It doesn't always mean— Oh, I give up!" Tasha snarled crossly.

"Stop bickering," Bianca said firmly. "We need a plan. I'm not having those rats steal the treasure from under our noses. Not after – not after..." She shuddered, and the other kittens looked at her sympathetically. Bianca was still a bit nervous and wobbly about small places after being stuck in the dolls' house all night. She was also very keen to get her revenge on the rats.

"But don't you see? It's the rats that make this so strange!" Tasha cried. "They wouldn't know about pirate stories. They don't read any history, all they care about is eating things."

"Eating things is important! There are whole books about the history of food, you know," Boris said loftily. "And before you ask, I might not have read them, but I've looked at the pictures. The curator in the History of Cookery department has shelves full, each of them more delicious than the last. And he shares his sandwiches with me sometimes. He's a very nice man."

"Tasha's got a point." Peter looked uncertainly up at Boris. "How would the rats find a treasure map?"

Boris thought for a moment. He so wanted to be right. Nothing exciting had happened in the museum for ages, it seemed to him. There had to be hidden treasure, and a map to find it by.

"The rats have tunnels all over the place," he said firmly. "Even more of them than us cats. You saw how quickly they disappeared off *The Silver Lion*! They couldn't have done that without some sort of shortcut – secret passageways full of secret hiding places full of secret treasure maps. Or one secret treasure map, at least. The rats didn't have to be clever to find the map, they probably just fell over it. Who knows what else they might have in their tunnels," he added thoughtfully.

"They don't deserve to have a treasure map," Bianca said, her whiskers bristling. "We have to get it off them."

"Mmmm." Boris flicked his tail from side to side. It was all very well saying that, but he wasn't quite sure how they were going to do it. He sneaked a glance sideways. Tasha was still looking doubtful and he had a feeling she was about to start arguing again. He couldn't have that. Much as he hated to admit it, Tasha was just a teensy bit smarter and sneakier than he was. He was going to need her help. "Don't worry." He stood up on top of the glass cabinet, raising his head high, and swishing his tail like a banner. "I have a plan!"

🐾 Chapter Four 🐾

"That's your plan? To follow the rats?"
Tasha said, her whiskers twitching with
disgust.

"Yes!" Boris had spent the rest of their
night in the Jewel Room thinking it up,
and he was quite proud of it. He gave
Tasha and the others a smug look and
went back to wolfing down his breakfast.

"I should have known. Last night,

when you said you were still working out the final details and you'd tell us in the morning, it just meant you didn't have a clue," Tasha snarled.

"Well, at least it's not complicated," Peter said, and both Tasha and Boris glared at him. "Simple plans are the best, usually…?" he trailed off. "Oh. Don't mind me."

Boris, Tasha and Bianca were brother and sisters, while Peter was an orphan who'd turned up at the museum in mysterious circumstances. Sometimes he wasn't quite sure which arguments he was allowed to join in…

"It's a perfectly good plan," Boris hissed, still glaring at Tasha. "The rats are bound to be carrying the map around with them, so how else are we going to get hold of it? And my plan isn't just to *follow* the rats anyway." He stuck his nose in the air. "We're going to follow the rats *sneakily*."

"It all sounds very sensible to me," Bianca said, coming to stand next to Boris. She rubbed the side of her head lovingly against his shoulder and twined her tail in and out of his. "I think we should set off after them right now. The sooner we get hold of that map, the sooner I can wrap myself up in rubies."

"You do know that even if there is any treasure – and I still don't think there is – we don't get to keep it," Tasha said.

Bianca's eyes widened. "Not even a tiny bit of it? Just one ruby? One or two?"

"No. It'll all belong to the museum."

"Oh…" Bianca drooped, her whiskers almost trailing the floor, and Boris glared at Tasha.

"Did you have to be so mean?" he whispered. "She's still upset about that dolls' house. She was enjoying thinking about jewels instead!"

Tasha eyed her sister guiltily. "Don't worry, Bianca. There'll still be all the glory. You might even get your picture in the newspaper."

Bianca recovered in seconds. She set

about a thorough wash, just in case there happened to be any photographers lurking about already.

"Come on then," Tasha muttered, relenting. "I suppose we'd better go and find those rats. It's almost opening time, but we might be able to track them down before the museum gets too busy."

They eventually caught up with the rats in the Ancient Greece Gallery. They were gathered in a ring around an enormous vase, painted with an octopus swirling its arms all over the sides. The octopus's huge eyes seemed to gaze out across the gallery, as if it was looking for something. It made Boris feel quite shuddery. All four rats were peering up at the vase as though it was the most fascinating thing they'd ever seen.

The kittens huddled behind a bronze statue, listening hard.

"What are they saying?" Boris whispered to Tasha. "They're too squeaky for me."

"Shhh!" Tasha hissed back. "Just let me listen!"

"I don't get it," the small grey rat said, wrinkling her nose.

"Why do you have to be so difficult, Dusty?" growled the big brown rat, who seemed to be in charge. He was looking between the vase and a brightly coloured piece of paper, and he seemed confused. "It's a sea monster, isn't it? Obviously it's a clue!"

"But the vase is ancient, boss. It came from Crete. Thousands of years old, this is. It can't be a clue to a treasure map that was made only a few centuries ago."

"Paws up for listening to Dusty, who's being clever on purpose?" the big rat snapped. The other two rats looked at each other and then at the big one, and kept still.

The big rat nodded smugly. "And paws up for listening to me, Luther, when I say that a great, big, enormous squid thing is obviously an important clue to understanding the treasure map. Because it's to do with the sea. Of course."

The other two rats gave Dusty an apologetic look and then put their paws up. After a moment, the littlest one put *both* paws up.

"Fine," muttered Dusty. "What does the clue mean then, boss?"

Luther stared at her, his eyes widening slightly. Then he looked back at the vase. "Oh. Um. Well, it's obvious, isn't it?"

"No." Dusty was so cross that her long pink tail was twitching from side to side. Luther fixed his beady black eyes on it as it coiled around.

"Well… It means…" He wrenched his eyes away from her writhing tail, snatched up the map and stared at the vase. "Aha! Look! It's pointing that way. The leg."

"Arm," Dusty muttered.

"Whatever. It's pointing towards the door, isn't it. Of course. So we need to go through there. Towards the café!" Luther charged off, with Pip and Morris scooting after him. The small grey rat looked up at the octopus vase and the eight arms pointing in eight different directions, and sighed. Then she followed after them with a quiet murmur of, "Give me strength…"

"I feel almost sorry for that poor rat," Tasha said, watching Dusty plod off after the others. "And it's quite clear they haven't the first idea what they're doing with that map – if it *is* a map. It looked a bit bright and shiny for something so old… They're only heading to the café because it's their favourite place for scrounging."

"Well, I'm feeling sorry for the big

one, even if he did crumple my whiskers when I crashed into him that time," Boris growled. "All that Dusty does is moan! It's very hard trying to have an adventure when some people keep pouring cold water on everything you say!"

"I was only explaining to you… Oh! Fine!" Tasha laid her ears back furiously. "Go on then. Tell us what to do now!"

"We must follow them! They could be halfway to the treasure already! Hurry up!"

Boris poked his nose out from behind the statue, checking the coast was clear, then dodged round an elderly lady admiring a red figure vase and shot across the gallery after the rats.

"This is making my whiskers ache,"

Tasha said to the statue. But she didn't want to be left behind. She caught up with Boris, Peter and Bianca outside the entrance to the café. The three kittens were lurking under a big board advertising the soup of the day, and watching the rats.

Boris looked round at her, his golden eyes glittering furiously. "They must have found a clue, look at them! They're celebrating! Why did you have to argue so much?"

"What?" Tasha blinked.

"Look!" Boris twitched his ears at the little knot of rats, hidden away in the shadows under a bin. The big brown rat, Luther, looked extremely smug, and all four of them were stomping around in a circle in a happy sort of dance. Something was definitely going right.

Tasha gasped. "Maybe they've worked out how to follow the map!"

"Yes! And now they're going to find our treasure!" Bianca mewed. "Oh, it just isn't fair! What are the rats even going to do with it? Rats don't like jewels and gold coins, they only want to eat things. You can't eat pearls!"

Tasha's eyes brightened. "Actually, Cleopatra, the Queen of Egypt, you know – she did once eat a pearl. But she had to dissolve it in vinegar first. And I'm not sure it would have tasted very nice."

"Now is not the time for stupid stories about Egypt!" Boris said crossly. "What are we going to do? We have to get hold of that map! We need to find the treasure before they do!"

"But do we?" Peter said thoughtfully. "If the treasure's got to go to the museum anyway, does it matter who finds it?"

"Do you want the rats to win?" Boris yowled, staring at Peter in shock. Then he realized what he'd done as several surprised visitors turned round to see what had made such an awful noise.

"Ooops… Anyway, even if we can't keep it, there's bound to be a reward for handing an enormous pile of treasure over to the museum, isn't there? A lifetime supply of those special prawn sandwiches perhaps? They might even *name* a sandwich after me," he added blissfully. "A Boris Baguette. Tuna and prawn with a touch of lemon, and none of those horrible salady bits…"

"Sandwiches? Have you been stealing sandwiches again, gingery one?" growled a hoarse old voice. The four kittens spun round to find Grandpa Ivan ducking under the board to join them, glaring down from one bright green eye. "And what was that dreadful howl I just heard from down in the cellars? Was that you too?"

"Sorry, Grandpa…" Boris hung his head. "But it's important – we're hunting for treasure!"

Chapter Five

"Sandwich treasure or actual treasure?"
Grandpa Ivan demanded keenly.

"Actual treasure! Honestly!" Boris
looked at Grandpa Ivan and his one eye.
He'd never thought about it before, but
if Grandpa wore a patch, he would look
exactly like a pirate. Perhaps he *was* a
pirate? A retired pirate? Boris gazed
admiringly at his grandfather. "Although

Tasha says that if we find it, we'll have to give it to the museum," he added sadly. "But there might be a reward, don't you think? A lifetime supply of prawn sandwiches?"

"And just a few rubies…" Bianca put in, her tail swishing from side to side in excitement. "Little ones."

"So what were you howling about?" Grandpa Ivan demanded.

Boris shuffled his paws and hung his head. "The rats have got the treasure map and we think they've worked out how to follow it," he admitted. "They're going to find the treasure before we even get a chance."

"And they won't look after it properly," Tasha put in, her eyes wide with worry.

"What if they try to eat the pearls? The museum isn't going to want them if they're rat-nibbled."

"Then we have to get that map. No rats will be nibbling treasure in MY museum," Grandpa Ivan hissed, and the ruff of white fur around his neck stood out like a lion's mane. "I forbid it."

"Oh." Boris looked up. "Oh good. Um, what does that actually mean, Grandpa? What are you going to do?"

"I'm too old for treasure-hunting." Grandpa Ivan sighed. "So I shall be handing over all responsibility for the search to my helpful and reliable grandkittens."

Boris twitched the very tip of his tail as he tried to work this out.

"That means us, doesn't it?" Tasha said glumly.

Grandpa Ivan leaned over and touched his whiskers to hers. "I'm sure you won't let me down, little tabby one. And you –" he glared sternly at Boris – "don't let those rats put so much as a paw on our treasure, you hear me?" Then he stalked out on to the terrace to sunbathe on the warm stone steps.

"Wonderful." Boris's shoulders sagged.

"If we don't find the treasure first, I'm going to be in trouble with Grandpa too. How did this all end up being my fault? All I did was see a sailing ship in the clouds…" He flattened his ears and stared grumpily at Tasha. "It was *you* who started it, going on about dragons."

Tasha nudged noses with him sympathetically and then her eyes widened. "Boris, look… The rats are on the move…"

The rats had scuttled out from under the bin. They were almost invisible as they hurried away, pressed against the shadows on the wall. The biggest rat was carrying the map in his mouth, rolled up like a scroll.

"After them!" Boris hissed. "But stay far enough back so they don't know that we're following. We don't want to put them on their guard…"

The rats' map didn't seem to have a very direct route to the treasure. The kittens spent the whole day chasing after them, all around the museum – in and out of the Dinosaur Gallery, the Roman Room, the Transport Galleries and half a dozen other exhibitions. The rats even popped into the little room with all the strange ear trumpets, and then dashed out looking extremely pleased with themselves.

The kittens, who had spent the night guarding the Jewel Room, not snoozing and snacking like the rats, were exhausted. The rats still had them chasing around past closing time – but at least now they didn't have to worry about running into visitors, they only had to worry about keeping out of the way of the Old Man who guarded the museum once everyone had gone home.

"I don't think they know what they're doing with that map!" Tasha complained as they crept after the rats into the Musical Instruments Room. "What's the point of dashing about here, there and everywhere? Maps are supposed to show you how to find things, not how not to find them!"

"Diamond Nell was a very cunning pirate," Boris huffed wearily. "I expect it's supposed to make treasure hunters give up. You only get to find the treasure if you're really, really determined."

"Do you think we could stop for a quick nap?" Peter suggested, swallowing an enormous yawn.

"No," Boris growled. "It's time for us to go on the offensive. No more of this mimsy following them about. We're going to ambush them right now and steal the map back."

"We can't steal it *back*," Tasha pointed out. "We never had it in the first place. It's the rats' map."

"No, it isn't. This is our museum, therefore it's our map. Simple." Boris planted his paws firmly, trying to look big and brave and determined.

"I wonder if the rats think it's *their* museum," Tasha said thoughtfully, but Peter gave a cross little sniff.

"They probably do, and they're wrong! We work for our living! All they do is steal and laze about. Boris is right – they don't deserve to have a treasure map."

"Exactly." Boris gave Peter an approving look.

The rats were investigating a very elderly looking instrument, rather like a piano, but painted gold all over. It had tall, spindly, curved legs, each one carved with a delicate golden hoof at the end, and the raised lid was painted with flowers.

As the cats watched, the big brown rat pointed to something on the map, and the very littlest one swarmed up one of the curved legs and ran across the keyboard, sending out a string of glittering notes. The little rat hopped up on the golden case, rubbing his paws together in glee. Then he thumped all the way back again, bouncing so hard that wooden pegs began to jump out of the top of the instrument.

"Oh *no!*" Tasha stood up, looking furious. "No! They'll break it! That harpsichord is nearly four hundred years old, they can't do that! Right. That's it! Boris! We have to get the map off them this minute. I don't care if the rats found it first. Imagine what they might do to that treasure."

Boris glared at her. "That's exactly what I just said," he huffed. "The problem is *how*? We've been following them all day – that big rat never lets go of it!"

His tabby sister curled her lip, showing her needle-sharp teeth. "Wait and see. Peter – you're the lightest of us. Do you think you could climb to the top of that harp?"

She fluttered her whiskers at a huge, heavily carved harp standing just behind the harpsichord.

Peter looked up at the harp, and then up again. It was very tall… But it was covered in carvings of fruit and flowers all the way up the frame. Lots of pawholds. "Yes…" he whispered. "Why?"

"Because from up there you'll be able to look down on the map," Tasha explained. "That big rat Luther has his paw on it, look. He's pointing out where they have to go next, but it's impossible to see from here. If we get wherever it is first—"

"We can ambush them!" Boris said, his eyes lighting up.

"Exactly!"

Peter nodded eagerly and hopped up

on to a large, carved golden pineapple
at the foot of the harp. The strings
thrummed faintly as he clambered up the
side, but luckily the rats were intent on
their map.

Peter clung to the carved scroll at the
very top of the harp and gazed down
at the sheet of paper, spread flat on the
floor. Luther was poring over it with
Morris, who was
clearly his second
in command, and
they were pointing
towards a drawing…
Peter leaned out
a little further to
see, and felt the harp
wobble underneath him.

It swayed sickeningly towards the rats and then back again. Peter closed his eyes and clung on as tightly as he could.

"He's going to fall!" Boris whispered frantically. He charged at the harp, sending it swinging back the other way. He could feel the tingle of the strings run through his fur and his whiskers stood on end. There was a horrible jangling chord and Boris hunched his shoulders, ready for the harp to collapse on his head.

"It's all right," Peter said, sliding down beside him. The two kittens slumped on the polished floor in a pile of fur. "You stopped it.

We're safe. Boris, you can open your eyes!"

"Did you see the map?" Boris whispered hoarsely, opening one eye a slit.

"Yes!" Peter nodded eagerly. "The big rat was pointing to a ship. I think they're about to head back to *The Silver Lion* – maybe the treasure's in one of those little tunnels they've got running through the ship?"

Bianca and Tasha came nosing anxiously at them, and Boris struggled up.

"Did they see Peter looking?" he asked his sisters.

"They heard you messing about with the harp, but I don't think they knew what you were doing," Tasha said, licking his nose gently.

Boris shook his ears excitedly. "Then we just have to get to the ship first!"

🐾 Chapter Six 🐾

"Are you ready?" Boris hissed from the bow, up near the lion figurehead with its silvery wooden mane. "Is everyone in position?"

Whispers came back from all around the ancient ship, and Boris pricked his ears proudly as he heard Peter say, "Aye aye, sir!"

The kittens still didn't know where the

rats' secret tunnels and entrances to *The Silver Lion* were, so Boris had split them up. As soon as anyone spotted the rats, they were to make the secret signal. Then hopefully one of the kittens would be able to grab the map from an unsuspecting rat. *Hopefully.*

Boris froze as little tapping footsteps sounded in the walls of the ship beside him. The rats were coming! Boris coughed a little to clear his throat and then hooted like an owl – or as much like an owl as he could. *More of a me-owl,* he thought, trying not to snigger. He was nervous…

The footsteps stopped for a moment and tiny, squeaky voices muttered behind the timbers, but then they scritched and scrabbled on towards him. Where were they coming from, exactly? Boris crouched next to the silver lion, his tail swelling up like a fat furry brush. Underneath, somewhere? Ah! A small, dark hole in the boarding. Could the rats really squeeze through that?

Boris glanced apologetically at the figurehead, then sprang on to its back, clinging to the carved curls of its mane. He held on as tightly as he could, leaning over the edge, his eyes fixed on the hole. The little footsteps tapped louder and louder underneath him, and all around the ship's rail, Tasha, Peter and Bianca came creeping closer, ready to leap to his aid.

All at once the rats burst out of the hole in the side of the ship, squeaking together in chattery excitement. And the big brown one had the map in his jaws!

Wait… Wait… Now!

Boris swooped down one massive ginger paw and whopped the map straight out of Luther's mouth. Then Tasha made a huge jump from the ship's rail, seizing the map in her teeth and darting away up the rigging.

Boris stared down gleefully at the rats. He was expecting fury, and rat howls, and angry paws clenched into fists – but none of that happened.

The big brown rat snorted loudly and yelled, "Too late, fur-face! We had you conned the whole time! Thought you were being clever, didn't you? Thought we hadn't noticed you clumping about after us?"

What did he mean? There was a sinking feeling in Boris's stomach.

"We were leading you on! We knew where the treasure was the whole time!" Luther smirked at Boris and the others, showing all of his long yellowish teeth.

"And now we're off to the museum shop to fetch it and you can't stop us!" added the littlest rat, and he blew a ratty raspberry back at the gaping cats.

All four rats sped away across the deck, chortling to each other, and disappeared through a spidery crack in the woodwork.

"They spotted us?" Boris turned to stare at the others. "No way!"

Tasha was holding the map pressed up against the ship's rigging, and staring at it. "Off to the museum shop to fetch the treasure," she said now. "Oh … oh no…"

"What?" Boris demanded anxiously. "Do you think we ought to call Grandpa Ivan and the others? Perhaps if we turn up at the shop in force we can chase the rats away. But it doesn't seem very heroic…"

"Don't worry," Tasha sighed. She took the map in her teeth again and clambered slowly down the rigging to the deck.

"We don't want the treasure all

nibbled!" Bianca said, staring at her. "What about my rubies?"

"There aren't any rubies," Tasha said sadly, stretching out the map in front of the other kittens. "I was right. Though I wish I wasn't. Look. This isn't a treasure map."

The four kittens studied the brightly coloured sheet in front of them. Boris stuck out a paw. "Yes, it is. Look. X marks the spot. It's definitely a treasure map."

"All right." Tasha nodded. "It's a *sort* of treasure map. But it's not old, and it's nothing to do with pirates. It's not the only one, either. There are hundreds like this piled up by the museum entrance. Haven't you seen children wandering around with them? You get a stamp on the map for each room you visit, and if you get to them all, you can go to the shop for a bag of gold coins." She heaved a huge sigh. "Gold *chocolate* coins."

Deep down under the marble floor of the Grand Hall, four delighted rats were speeding towards the museum shop.

"Chocolate! I love chocolate!" squealed

Dusty. "We hardly ever find chocolate left behind."

"After all that whinging you did about my brilliant map-reading, you don't deserve any chocolate," Luther told her. "Lucky for you I'm such a wise and generous leader."

"I'm still not sure we needed to go to all those different rooms," Dusty said thoughtfully.

"We were following the map. Maps are important. Anyway, exercise is good for you." Luther sniggered happily to himself. "We led those horrible little cats a proper chase, didn't we?"

Morris snorted. "Did you see them, trying to sneak around behind us? Mind you, boss, I did think the black one was going to squash Pip when he fell off that stringy thing."

The littlest rat bared his teeth fiercely. "No way! I'd have bitten him on the bottom, boss!"

"You know what makes it so much better?" Dusty said, stopping for a moment to catch her breath and preen her silky whiskers. "Cats don't even like chocolate!"

🐾 Chapter Seven 🐾

"You mean, there never was any treasure?" Boris asked miserably.

"Not really." Tasha's whiskers were drooping too. She was being quite nice about it all, Boris thought. If it had been him, he wouldn't have been able to resist crowing *I told you so*. "I mean, there are the chocolate coins. But no rubies or pearls or anything like that."

"We spent the whole day racing around the museum after those horrible rats, for chocolate?" Bianca shrieked. "CHOCOLATE? That sweet sticky stuff that gums up your fur?"

"It isn't that bad," Boris muttered. "Although I'd rather have a prawn sandwich, obviously."

"Chocolate is poisonous to cats, Boris," Tasha said, her voice weary.

"Oh." Boris looked mildly worried for a moment. "Is it? Well, I never noticed. I have quite a strong stomach."

"I suppose at least we can have a nap now." Peter let out an enormous, jaw-breaking yawn. "Shall we go back down to the cellars? It feels like days since I saw a nice comfy bed."

The others nodded and began to trail slowly across the deck towards the gangway.

"I might just stay here and sleep," Boris said. Somehow, he didn't feel like going downstairs to curl up with the others. He felt rather foolish. He wanted to be on his own for a while.

"Are you sure, Boris?" Tasha called, her muzzle wrinkling a little in worry.

"Yes…" Boris jumped up on to the ship's rail and padded round to the top of the silver lion figurehead. He slumped gloomily on to the carved mane, and glared out along the bowsprit. Pirates. Treasure. How could he have been so silly?

There was an eerie creaking noise underneath him, and Boris froze. Were

the rats back?
What *was* that?
Was it a creak
or was it …
a roar?
An ancient,
tired, wooden
roar?

Boris stood up,
very slowly, and edged
away from the lion's mane.

Tasha came racing back along the
deck and leaped up on to the ship's rail,
with Bianca and Peter scrambling after
her. "What was that noise? Oh, Boris!
Please say you haven't broken it?" She
looked down at her paws and then
around the ship, as if she expected it to

fall to pieces under her.

"All I did was sit down!" Boris said defensively. "I mean, I might have sat a little bit hard, but still … it's a ship. It isn't supposed to be delicate. It ought to be able to stand up to a kitten."

"Like that tyrannosaurus? This ship is hundreds of years old. We're supposed to be gentle." Tasha sighed. "Look! You made a *hole* in it! Oh no!"

"Ah." Boris looked down at the lion's wooden mane. Tasha was right. There between his ginger and white front paws was a small, dark hole in the carving. "Um. Are you sure it wasn't there before?"

"I don't know, was it?" Tasha hissed. "I don't think it was – didn't you hear that roaring noise?"

"Yes," Boris admitted. He patted the hole with one paw, trying to push the bits of wood back together. They didn't budge. "It's not very big. Perhaps no one will notice," he said hopefully, looking round at the others.

"It's the sort of thing they do notice round here," Peter said. "They're quite fussy about holes in things. Especially when they weren't there before."

Boris peered down at the hole, his eyes worried slits. "You know, I think there's something in there."

"Don't touch it!" Tasha squeaked. "Don't make it worse! What if the whole ship falls apart?"

"Like a self-destruct button?" Boris looked round at her. "Did pirate ships have those?"

"I don't know! Let's not find out!"

Tasha was probably right, Boris knew
that. But all the same… He wanted to
know. "It looks more like a
bit of paper," he said – and
then he stuck his paw
in, and hooked it out.

"Boris! Historical
artefact! No claws!"
Tasha squeaked, but
she leaned closer to
see what it was.

Carefully, and trying
to use only the pink pads
of his paws, Boris flattened out
the folded piece of paper. It was thick and
old, yellowish and water-stained, and the

ink was a faded brown. In the middle
of the piece of paper was
a large, dark X.

🐾 Chapter Eight 🐾

"Now that is definitely a treasure map,"
Boris said smugly.

"I think you're right," Tasha breathed.

"Are you sure?" Bianca scowled at the
paper. "I don't want to waste any more
time running around the museum on a
wild goose chase, thank you very much."

"It's definitely old," Peter pointed out.
"Look how ragged it is. All those stains

and marks."

"Look at the X!" Boris said, his eyes glittering with excitement. "Have you ever seen anything that looks more like a secret treasure map? It's the real thing, all right!" He squinted at the map sideways. "Mind you… I'm not absolutely sure what it says."

"Let's get back down to the cellars," Tasha suggested. "We don't want the rats to realize what's going on. I know they were happy about the chocolate, but if they knew there was real treasure, I wouldn't put it past them to try and get the map – I mean, we did steal theirs…"

Boris held the map carefully in his teeth and the kittens streamed back down the gangway and through the darkened museum to the cats' lair in the cellars. There they snuggled up on the pile of old tapestries to take a proper look at Boris's find.

The map was a tattered square of thick paper, very yellowed and brittle. The kittens gazed at it in awe. There was definitely an "X marks the spot" but it wasn't very clear what it was marking. The map was full of strange dotted lines and squiggles and blotches. It was a bit hard to tell what was part of the original map, and what was just dirt.

"I can't tell what it's a map of," Tasha said. She put out a paw and turned the map round to see if it looked better the other way up. It didn't.

The kittens looked at each other, their noses wrinkled – finally they'd found a treasure map, but they couldn't work out how to use it!

"Supper time, kittens."

Boris scooted the map quickly under his tummy, and looked up at their mother with innocent golden eyes. He tried to, anyway. He didn't do it very well. Unfortunately he was one of those kittens who always seemed to look guilty. But he didn't want to hand over their precious map to Ma and the other cats now – he knew what would happen. It would be too important for *kittens* to deal with, even though they were the ones who had found it!

"What have you done?" Smoke asked suspiciously. "I know that face, Boris. Have you broken something? Please say it wasn't anything valuable."

"I haven't!" Boris protested. Then he remembered the hole in *The Silver Lion*, and shuffled his paws a bit. "Not much…"

His mother groaned. "I'm not sure I want to know. But I can't hear any museum staff having hysterics, or not yet. Come and eat."

"The museum staff are going to be delighted," Tasha said, rubbing the top of her head into her mother's chin. "I promise, Ma."

For once Boris wasn't hungry. Not very hungry, anyway. He ate quite slowly, still trying to puzzle out those strange marks and scribbles on the map, until Tasha nudged him mid-mouthful.

"What?"

"Ma's got her eye on you. She's looking worried. Eat something!"

Boris tried to gobble, but his heart wasn't in it. He didn't stay to lick out the dishes the way he usually did, either.

"We'll have to think about it overnight," he muttered to the others as he carefully tucked the map away underneath a fold of their tapestry bed. "We must find a way to work it out! We have to!"

Upstairs in the museum shop, four hopeful rats popped out of a tiny hole in the floorboards and peered around, their whiskers twitching.

"So where is it then?" Luther demanded. "It says on this map that we get the chocolate coins from the shop."

"I can smell chocolate, I know I can," muttered Morris, swarming up the side of the counter and scurrying about.

"Is it up there?" Luther called eagerly.

"Yes, boss. Um, boss…?" Morris said. He was standing with his front paws pressed against a glass-fronted cabinet, his nose squashed up against the glass as he tried to see inside.

"What?" Luther snapped back, his eyes glinting dangerously. "I found the chocolate."

"Excellent!"

"I don't suppose that map says anything about how to get into a locked cupboard?"

Worn out after the night shift and the busy day of searching, Boris slept late, but Tasha hooked the map out from under the tapestries and the other three kittens stared at it, frowning.

"Do you think it's a map of the ship?" Peter asked, squinting.

"I hope so." Tasha sighed. "We don't have a hope if it isn't, do we? I mean what if it's a map of a treasure island? We can't go sailing off somewhere!"

"Couldn't we?" Bianca asked wistfully.

"No! Anyway, think of all that sand getting in your fur, you'd hate it. And seawater too!"

"I suppose so." Bianca sniffed at the map.

"What does it smell of? It's strange…"

Tasha and Peter sniffed, and even Boris half rolled over in his sleep and sniffed at the grubby paper.

"Mmmm … tuna…" he murmured.

"It does not smell of tuna, Boris," Tasha said crossly, but Boris was still almost asleep and didn't answer her, since he was dreaming of breakfast. Instead, he stretched out his long pink tongue and started to lick the map, lapping at it delicately, as if it really was the very nicest tuna.

"Boris, stop it!" Tasha hissed in horror. "You'll damage the map, stop!"

"Mmm, what? What's that?" Boris half opened his eyes, gazing around at them dozily. "Is it breakfast time? Did I oversleep?"

"You were licking a historical artefact!" Tasha growled at him. "You could have ruined it!"

"More to the point, you might have licked off the ink and then we'd never be able to find the treasure," Bianca said.

"It's my map," Boris said haughtily. "You should have woken me up if you were going to look at it."

"Hang on a minute." Peter was peering down at the map. "Look at where he licked it. There's more lines there now.

And some of those squiggles look like letters."

Boris woke up properly and gave the map a hopeful look. "Yes! There are words now – doesn't that say *tail*? And there, I'm sure that word is *stars*… Oh, but they're fading away again!"

"Maybe we need to get it properly wet," Peter suggested.

Tasha gave a faint little squeak of horror. "But it's a precious historical document—" she started to say, and then her whiskers drooped as the others glared at her and Boris hissed, "Treasure map, Tasha!"

"Oh, I suppose..."

"The fountain! We can go and dip it in the fountain." Boris sprang up. "Quick – there's not long before the museum opens, we don't want loads of visitors wondering what we're doing."

The kittens rushed up the spiral staircase to the tiny door under the cat statue. The fountain was in the centre of the courtyard garden in front of the museum – it was a lovely place to sit, with the cool spray of the water misting

around on a hot day. Now, early in
the morning, the garden was deserted
except for one or two of the older cats
wandering here and there.

The four kittens leaped up on to the
rim of the fountain, and Boris leaned
over, ready to dip the map into the
marble bowl.

"Just what are you kittens doing?"

"Ma!" Boris squeaked round his mouthful of map. He swayed back and forth on the edge of the fountain, desperately trying to recover his balance. "You can't sneak up behind someone standing next to a bowl of water! I nearly went in!" He hopped down on to the paving stones, shaking his whiskers indignantly, and the other kittens followed him, looking innocently at their mother and Grandpa Ivan, who had come up beside her.

"You're all banned from going anywhere near that fountain, after the last time Boris fell in it and slopped water over half the museum's nicely polished floors!" Smoke snapped. "With help from your sister, I seem to remember."

"Oh, Ma…" Boris and Bianca moaned at exactly the same time.

Grandpa Ivan leaned closer, peering at Boris with one bright green eye. "What's that in your mouth?"

"We need to –" Tasha started to say, and then she remembered that the map was a secret and looked guilty.

"You need to what?" Smoke narrowed her eyes. "What are you four doing? Boris, what *is* that bit of paper in your mouth?"

"Nothing!" the kittens chorused, all trying to get between Boris and Smoke and hide the map.

"It's the café menu!" Boris spluttered. "I was so hungry! I thought it might

keep me going for a bit!" Tasha stared
hard at Grandpa Ivan and then looked
meaningfully at the map in Boris's mouth.
Grandpa had been so keen on them
finding the treasure. Perhaps he could
help out now? Had the old white cat's
whiskers flickered a message? Or had she
imagined it?

"Tch…" Grandpa Ivan sighed. "Leave the kittens to me, my dear. You're on duty tonight. Go and rest. I'll give them a piece of my mind."

"Hmmm," Smoke muttered, but she stalked away, leaving the kittens gazing gratefully at their grandfather.

"We found it! The treasure map, Grandpa, look!" Boris spat the map out at Grandpa Ivan's feet and looked up at him proudly.

"Goodness me," Grandpa Ivan murmured, peering down at it. "So what on earth were you doing hopping around on the fountain? Why aren't you after the treasure?"

"Because we think the map needs to get wet," Peter explained. "More writing

showed up when Boris licked it, you
see. We were going to dip it in the
fountain."

"Ah… Secret disappearing ink!"
Grandpa Ivan sounded impressed. He
sat down next to the map and curled
his tail thoughtfully around his paws.
"Well … your mother may have banned
you from the fountain, but I didn't
hear her say anything about the
river."

"The river! But … Grandpa…"
Tasha padded closer to
Grandpa Ivan, nudging
him worriedly with
her nose.
"I mean …
the river…"

Soon after Peter had turned up at the museum as a bedraggled foundling, Grandpa Ivan had told the kittens the story of his own arrival. He had been thrown into the river in a sack, many years before, and he had only survived when a child pulled him out on to the bank by the museum. He had been left with a deep fear of water – and now he wanted them to go to the river?

"Mmm…" Grandpa Ivan looked thoughtfully towards the river, out of sight beyond the museum buildings, and shuddered. "No one ever said treasure-hunting was easy, kittens."

"We'll be careful, Grandpa." Boris stood up straighter, puffing out his ginger chest. "I promise. I won't let them get into any trouble."

Tasha, Bianca and Peter exchanged a glance behind Boris's back, but they didn't say anything. Grandpa was right. They were treasure hunters now. Brave and daring.

Weren't they?

🐾 Chapter Nine 🐾

"It's very big," Tasha said, gazing nervously at the river stretching out in front of them. She stepped back a little, not wanting her paws so close to all that water.

"It is…" Boris agreed. He glanced round at the reassuring bulk of the museum, just across the gardens.

"Do you think it's deep?" Peter asked, watching the dark water hurry by.

"I don't like it," Bianca whispered. "Let's go back!"

"It's all right as long as we don't go too near," Tasha soothed her.

"But remember Grandpa Ivan's story," Bianca said, shuddering. "Tied up in a sack, and thrown into this very river. Please let's go back."

"No," Boris told her firmly. "There's nothing bad about the river, Bianca. It was the cruel people who threw Grandpa into it who were wrong." He shook himself. "The water isn't frightening. Look, it sparkles in the sun, just like the fountain does." He nodded at the glittering ripples.

"There's a lot more of it here than there is in the fountain," Bianca muttered. But she did lean out a little to gaze at the shining water.

"And just look at those boats…" Boris sighed admiringly. "Just imagine being out there, the wind ruffling your fur… I do like things with engines."

"Boris, look!" Peter had been lying stretched out on the paving, gazing down into the water, and now his tail was swishing excitedly from side to side.

"Little fishes! Tiny ones!"

All the kittens leaned out over the edge to see. Shoals of tiny fish were zipping around in the dark greenish water, clouds of them gleaming silver where they caught the light.

"Swimming snacks..." Boris murmured, leaning out slightly too far. "OW!" He turned round to glare at Bianca, who'd stamped down hard on his tail.

"You were about to fall in! Those are not prawn sandwiches, Boris! You don't know how to catch fish."

"I bet I could learn," Boris said sulkily, but he did shuffle back a bit. "Anyway. We aren't here to catch fish, we're supposed to be solving this treasure map. Where is it?"

There was a moment of panic as four kittens looked for the map, before they realized that Boris had been sitting on it ever since they arrived at the river's edge. Boris took it carefully in his teeth, and leaned cautiously out to dip it into the water.

"Don't leave it in too long!" Tasha said anxiously. "We don't want it to fall apart."

Boris backed up hurriedly, laying the

map on the warm paving slabs, and the kittens stared down at it.

"Did it work?" Boris asked, shaking water off his whiskers.

"Yes!" Tasha squeaked. "Yes, look! It's changing!"

Before their eyes, the lines on the map were growing and joining together, bleeding into each other to form shapes and words.

"What is that?" Bianca asked, turning her head from side to side. "It looks like a whole lot of boxes. It doesn't look like a ship at all. Oh, what if the treasure's miles and miles and miles away?"

"It's like the plans the visitors use to find their way round the museum," Tasha said, squinting at the map.

"It's not another thing for finding chocolate coins, is it?" Bianca wailed.

"No, no. This map is definitely old." Tasha pressed the edge of the map down with her paw. "Is that a cat there?" she asked, her whiskers tickling a cat-like shape drawn at the end of the strange boxes.

"It IS the ship!" Boris suddenly yelped. "It's *The Silver Lion* – that's not a cat, it's a lion. It's the figurehead at the bow, and the boxes are the holds."

Peter looked up at him. "The what?"

"The holds, the storage chambers down in the bottom of the ship. Where all the cargo went." Boris gave a happy sigh. "You need space for great boxes full of treasure."

"If it was that big, I think someone would have found it by now," Tasha said doubtfully.

Bianca's whiskers shivered with excitement. "It must mean that it's a very small, precious treasure. Diamonds and rubies don't take up a lot of room. Ooooh, are those words appearing? What do they say?"

Boris looked down at the map. "*The little bear's tail ... in the belly of the serpent...* What does that mean? Oh, please don't let it be a riddle. I'm no good at word games."

Tasha crouched down closer, her ears twitching with delight. Someone had once left a book of crosswords on a bench in the museum gardens, and it was one of her most treasured possessions. She loved to read the clues, over and over.

"Oh, how exciting. I wonder what it means."

"Honestly. It's already written in secret disappearing ink, do we really need mystery words as well?" Boris muttered. "I thought the great big cross would tell us where to look."

"That's the problem, I think." Tasha glanced up at him. "The cross is huge. It covers the whole of that front square. So the treasure could be anywhere in that hold." Then she gasped. "The words are disappearing again – I think they only appear while the paper's wet, and it's drying out again in the sun. Quick, we have to remember them before they go. Maybe the ink only works once!"

The kittens chanted together, "*The lion's nose points to the little bear's tail in the belly of the serpent. From the ladder walk ten paces to three.*"

"It's all very well remembering it," Bianca said, after they'd repeated it three times. "We still don't know what it means. It's gobbledegook."

"The ladder must be the ladder that leads down into the hold, I suppose," Boris mused.

"And the lion could be the figurehead!" Peter yelped.

"Or just the bow of the ship," Boris agreed. "And that would be the same thing anyway, since the figurehead is on the bow. That must be it!"

"Where do the bear and the serpent come in, though?" Tasha asked. "I'm sure I know something about the little bear, I just can't quite pin it down."

Boris looked over at the museum and sighed. "It must be well past opening time now. We're going to have to wait for closing time, aren't we? We can't go exploring around *The Silver Lion* with visitors everywhere." Then he groaned. "And we'll probably be on duty tonight. Where are we meant to be?"

Tasha wrinkled her nose happily. "On the ship. I told Ma I was very interested in nautical history and please could we swap."

Boris leaned over and brushed his whiskers into hers. "You *clever* kitten."

All day, Boris and Tasha and Peter and Bianca kept puzzling over the clues on the map. Were the bear and the serpent part of the carved decorations on the ship, perhaps? But Boris was sure he'd never seen them, and he'd wandered all over the great ship, imagining himself a pirate cat in times gone by.

Tasha was still trying to remember why the little bear sounded so familiar. She even nipped up to the Dolls' Houses and Toys Gallery, in case it was something about a teddy bear, but then she remembered that teddy bears hadn't been invented when *The Silver Lion* was afloat. She did see a grey-furred rat skulking around the gallery – Dusty bared her teeth and hissed furiously. It didn't look as if the rats had managed to find their chocolate treasure, either. But that didn't cheer Tasha up as much as she'd thought it would.

"What are you looking so miserable for, small stripy kitten?" Grandpa Ivan growled in her ear as she slunk back down to the cellars. "Don't tell me Boris dropped that map in the river?"

"Of course I didn't!" Boris said indignantly as Peter and Bianca snorted with laughter. "It's right here, look. But it's all written in riddles and it doesn't make sense."

"It's a mystery," Tasha put in, "and we can't solve it. We thought maybe you could help..."

The old white cat sat up a little straighter, and fluffed out his tail. "Ah, well. I am an international cat of mystery, after all. Tell me everything."

Chapter Ten

That night, Grandpa Ivan and the four kittens crept on to the deck of *The Silver Lion* and headed for the ladders leading down into the cabins just below. The holds were another floor down, Boris had explained. When *The Silver Lion* was afloat, they would have been underwater.

After they had shown Grandpa Ivan the clues, he had been so excited that his whiskers stood out like a great white fan. "Shiver me timbers…" he muttered. "I've never been much of a fan of ships, all that water, you know. Very … wet. But pirate treasure! Excellent work, my kittens. A real treasure map!"

"Do you know what it means, though?" Tasha had asked hopefully, and this time the white whiskers twitched with smugness.

"I might. I might indeed, little tabby one. You wait and see. Tonight, once all the visitors have gone, you can take me on to your ship, and we shall see what we shall see." Then he'd looked at them seriously. "But I shan't do any finding of treasure. It's your discovery, small ones, don't you worry. I'm only assisting with the map-reading."

Boris had never felt so proud. He was leading the other kittens – and Grandpa Ivan, the great adventurer! – deep down into the ship. He was the one who had found the map and now they were searching for treasure... He couldn't help strutting a little as they crossed the deck.

"Ladders..." Bianca said, peering doubtfully down into the darkness. "I don't like ladders."

Boris took a deep breath and tried not to shout at his sister. It would slow everyone down. "Don't worry," he said cunningly. "You just stay here. We can tell you about the treasure afterwards."

Bianca stuck her nose in the air. "I never said I wasn't going to go down the ladder. Just that I don't like them."

"Front paws first or back paws first?" Peter asked. "It's pretty steep."

"Front paws are best," Grandpa Ivan said. "Backwards is tricky."

The ladder didn't go straight down, thankfully. It was set on an angle, but the gaps still yawned wide between each step. Boris leaned over, and then reached his front paws down to see what it felt like. It was a long stretch, and he was taller than the other kittens. He swung his back paws down to join the front paws with a bump. "I think you have to do it in little hops," he called up to the others.

"Be careful!" Tasha mewed. "The steps might have rotted through."

Boris shuddered, and dabbed the next rung of the ladder with one paw before he put his weight on it. But it seemed quite solid. "It's all right! I'm nearly there." He hopped a couple more rungs, and then jumped on to the creaky wooden floor. "You can come down now, it's safe."

One by one, the
kittens came skittering
down the ladder, with
Grandpa Ivan last of all,
cautiously tiptoeing from step
to step.

"This is where the cabins
would have been," Boris explained.
"The next floor down is the hold. I've
looked at all the photos in the displays –

the hold has boards across it to divide it into compartments. I think we need to be in the front one."

"Come on then," Grandpa Ivan said briskly. "Mind you, once I'm down there I'm not sure I'm ever getting up again, but I wouldn't miss this for the world."

The kittens exchanged worried looks. If Grandpa Ivan got stuck, they were going to be in massive trouble. Still, Boris thought, hopefully they would have found the treasure before they had to tell anyone. That might cheer everyone up a bit.

The second ladder down to the hold was even steeper. This time Bianca decided to go down nose first in one go, and landed in a heap – but she landed on Boris, which everyone else seemed to think wasn't a problem.

"Which way now?" Boris asked, shaking himself grumpily. Why did everything always fall on top of *him*? "Grandpa? Have you worked out what all that stuff about bears and serpents means?"

"Aha!" Grandpa Ivan sat down at the bottom of the ladder, his white coat gleaming in the darkness of the hold. "How much do you kittens know about celestial navigation?"

All the kittens gazed back at him blankly. Then Tasha said slowly, "There's a celestial globe in the Maritime Gallery. It doesn't have countries on it – it has patterns of stars instead. Is it something to do with that?"

"Exactly!" Grandpa Ivan growled

delightedly. "Good work, stripy one. It means finding your way by the stars. Sailors have been doing it for centuries."

"It doesn't mention stars on that map," Bianca argued.

"No, but the Little Bear and the Serpent are the names of constellations – stars that cluster together and look like pictures. Those two are next to each other – in fact the Serpent wraps around the Little Bear."

"Yes! That's where I'd heard of the Little Bear!" Tasha purred. "So the Little Bear *is* in the Serpent's belly? But what does it mean? We can't see the stars from down here in the hold."

"Ah, well. The clue says that the lion's nose points to the Little Bear's tail. The star at the end of the Little Bear's tail is the most important one in the sky, for sailors. Polaris. The North Star."

"Sailors used it to navigate!" Boris jumped up excitedly. "That's on one of the displays in the Maritime Gallery too."

Grandpa Ivan nodded. "The North Star shows where true north is – it stands almost exactly above the North Pole."

Boris shook his whiskers. "I still don't see how that tells us where the treasure is. If the ship's moving around, it could be pointing in any direction. It doesn't make sense, talking about north. And where do the ten and three come in?"

"I think whoever hid the treasure was thinking of the compass points," Grandpa Ivan said slowly. "North is always at the top. Then if you move round the circle of a compass clockwise, you get to east, then south, then west and back up to north. So … east on the face of a compass is where you would find the number three on a clock face."

"Hang on…" Boris squeezed his eyes tight shut as he thought. "If the lion's nose is pointing north – that means the bow of the ship is north. And we have to stand where we are now at the bottom of the ladder, and walk ten paces towards three o'clock, or east."

"But probably not cat paces," Tasha put in. "We don't know who made the map and how long their legs were." She sighed. "*This* is why it's so important to have standard systems of measurement."

"Treasure, Tasha. Not mathematics," Boris snapped. "Ten paces that way! Just imagine one of the visitors, or the Old Man. Ten paces towards the east side of the ship!"

The five cats hopped as well as they could in human-sized steps across the hold.

"We're going to hit the side," Peter said, as they got to eight. "We'll have our noses up against the wall."

"Yes, against that piece of wood holding the planking together," Boris said, his eyes glittering in the darkness. "It's definitely in a straight line from the base of the ladder." He put his front paws up on the frame of the ship, looking hopefully for gaps between the frame and the planking. He might see the watery gleam of diamonds hidden away there, or gold coins shining...

"There!" he yelped, shoving hard with a front paw against a cloth-wrapped package that was sticking out behind the timber. The little parcel flew out the other side and landed on the boards with a thump.

"That doesn't look very sparkly," Bianca said dolefully.

Tasha nosed at the little parcel, pushing the cloth wrapping aside. "It looks like a book."

"A *book*?" Bianca wailed. "A book is all very well, Tasha, but it's nothing like rubies!"

Boris sighed. He had a feeling Bianca was right. All this fuss and effort for a book?

"A book could be a better treasure than any jewels," Grandpa Ivan said. "But we need a clearer light to look at it in. Boris, bring your treasure in your mouth. Let's see if I can get back up these ladders in one piece…"

Back in the cellars, Grandpa and the kittens ducked round behind the pile of tapestries to examine their treasure in secret. Boris laid the tatty little book out on the cloth, and stared down at it. It didn't look very exciting, even Tasha had to admit. Boris poked it with one paw, pushing it open, and they eyed the closely scrawled pages.

"Hang on…" Boris pushed his nose close up against the words. "Doesn't that say Boris?"

Tasha put her head on one side. "Definitely. Um… *Boris the ship's cat shared my hammock again the night gone.*" She looked round at the others excitedly. "It's a diary! From someone on *The Silver Lion*!"

"A true historical document," Grandpa Ivan boomed excitedly. "Smoke! Come and see what your clever kittens have found!"

"Still not as good as rubies," came a small mutter from Bianca, but the older museum cats were starting to gather around now. The kittens shuffled their paws and looked pleased as Smoke and Herring and the others sniffed at the diary, reading a few words here and there. Almost all the museum cats had lived in the great building all their lives – they knew how important a diary could be for finding out about the past. The kittens had made a great find.

"This is why you've all been hurrying around looking so suspicious for the last few days?" their mother murmured. "I had a horrible feeling you might have broken something again." She purred delightedly and licked Boris's ears. "That was a treasure map you were trying to hide from me!"

"Yes, and we solved the riddle! And now we know that the ship had a cat called Boris," Boris said, preening. "Not surprising really. It's a very historical name. Very important."

"He's never going to shut up about it, is he?" Peter muttered to Tasha.

"Do you think the museum will give me prawn sandwiches for life, when we show it to the staff?" Boris asked, looking hopefully at Smoke and Grandpa Ivan.

"Or maybe some rubies?" Bianca added.

Smoke nudged noses with him. "Maybe not for life, Boris dearest. But I reckon that diary is definitely worth a good fish supper. We must work out exactly where to leave it for the right staff to find. And perhaps you kittens should be sitting next to it, looking hungry..."

"Just think," Peter murmured to Boris and the others. "If you and Tasha hadn't seen ships and dragons up in the clouds, we might never have known there was treasure on board *The Silver Lion*."

"We might not even have found the treasure map," Tasha agreed.

Boris eyed the crowd of curious cats

around the diary, and fanned out his whiskers proudly. He had been right all along. Just for once…

Author's Note

The Silver Lion is based on a real ship with a lion figurehead – she's actually called the *Vasa*. She was built between 1626 and 1628, and she was a warship – or she was meant to be. She sank on her very first voyage, after sailing about 1300 metres! The whole ship tipped right over on one side, and she sank in minutes, with the sad loss of thirty sailors. She was underwater for more than 300 years, until she was rescued from Stockholm harbour in Sweden back in 1961. There's an amazing amount of the ship still in one piece, and you can see her in a fabulous museum in Stockholm.

In Chapter Ten, Tasha says how important it is to have proper ways to measure things. That was really important for the *Vasa*. There are lots of ideas about why the ship sank, but a few years ago, an archaeologist at the Vasa Museum found four of the rulers that the shipbuilders were using. Two of them were marked out in Swedish feet, and two of them in Amsterdam feet. An old Amsterdam foot had one more inch in it than a Swedish foot! So it's no wonder that the ship was a bit wobbly…

This is the Little Bear, or Ursa Minor – actually I always think it looks more like a saucepan. Another name for it is the Little Dipper – a dipper is a scoop for fetching water out of a barrel. The star at the end of the bear's tail, or the dipper's handle, is called Polaris. This is the North Star, the star that stands above true north. For thousands of years sailors have used the North Star to help them find their way home.

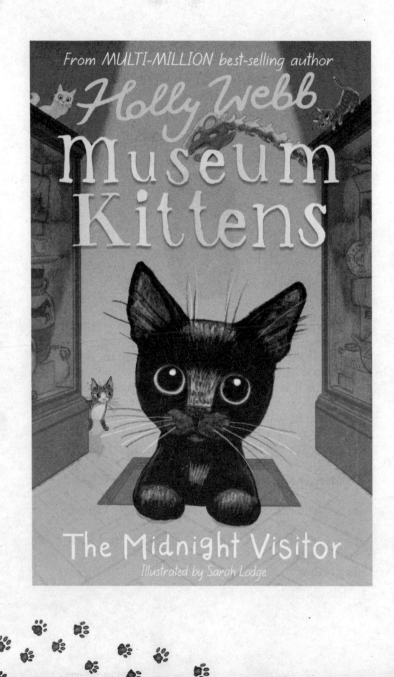

From MULTI-MILLION best-selling author

Holly Webb

Museum
Kittens

The Midnight Visitor

Illustrated by Sarah Lodge

One stormy night
a little black kitten is left
on the museum steps.

Tasha is eager to show Peter
the hidden passages and secret
corners, though not all the
kittens are so welcoming.

The pair set out to catch the
rat that's been stealing from the
Dinosaur Gallery. But when they
have a spine-chilling run-in with
a tyrannosaurus, will anyone
come to their rescue?

From MULTI-MILLION best-selling author

Holly Webb

Museum
Kittens

The Pharaoh's Curse

Illustrated by Sarah Lodge

The kittens are curious when
a rare Egyptian treasure is brought
to the museum.

From the moment the object arrives,
rumours of an ancient curse begin
to spread. But Tasha is determined
to prove to the other kittens that
there's nothing to be afraid of.

Then a pipe bursts and the
gallery is flooded – the kittens are
trapped! Are they the latest victims
of the pharaoh's curse?

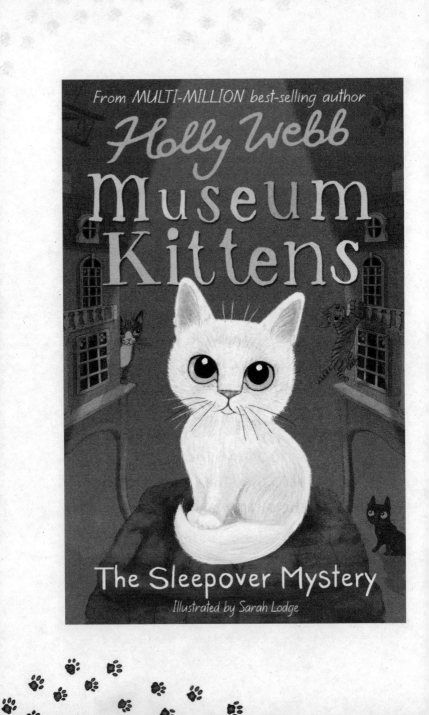

From MULTI-MILLION best-selling author

Holly Webb

Museum Kittens

The Sleepover Mystery

Illustrated by Sarah Lodge

The kittens can't wait to welcome a group of school children to the museum's first ever sleepover! Especially Bianca, who loves people fussing over her.

So when Bianca goes missing after a squabble with the other kittens, they worry that she has run away with the children.

But the rats have been sniffing around the sleepover too. Could the kittens' old enemies be behind Bianca's disappearance?

HOLLY WEBB

Holly Webb started out as a children's book editor and wrote her first series for the publisher she worked for. She has been writing ever since, with over one hundred books to her name. Holly lives in Berkshire, with her husband and three children. Holly's pet cats are always nosying around when she is trying to type on her laptop.

For more information
about Holly Webb visit:

www.holly-webb.com